You're a little monster

First published in Great Britain in 1998 by
Macdonald Young Books
an imprint of Wayland Publishers Ltd
61 Western Road
Hove
East Sussex
BN3 1JD

Text copyright © Sally Grindley 1998
and illustrations copyright © Arthur Robins 1998

Find Macdonald Young Books on the internet at http://www.myb.co.uk

Printed and bound in Belgium by Proost International Book Co.
British Library Cataloguing in Publication Data available.

ISBN: 0 7500 2365 1

SALLY GRINDLEY
You're a little mOnster

I've heard there might be a little monster living here.

Illustrated by Arthur Robins

MACDONALD YOUNG BOOKS